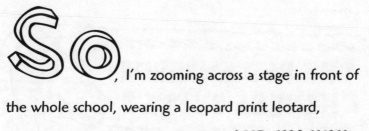

So, I'm zooming across a stage in front of the whole school, wearing a leopard print leotard, I've got soggy noodles on my head, AND MY **MUM** IS SINGING IN A TUTU.

How did I get here? Let's go back to the beginning...

I'm in

THE RED EMPEROR
CHINESE BUFFET

my favourite restaurant in the whole world EVER...

It's an all-you-can-eat buffet – like a regular

restaurant, EXCEPT the food is laid out like a buffet

and, you've guessed it, you can eat all you want! Yum!

My lovely family are all there, including **GRANNY**.

I have even managed to sneak

my beloved pet mouse

SCRIBBLES along with me.

SCRIBBLES

GOOD TIMES...

Well, it should be – but actually it's...

BAD TIMES!

Mabel has INSISTED on bringing her 'new best friend'
Richard along – they claim to like doing their
homework together and visiting museums,
but I suspect he might be her BOYFRIEND.

Scribbles has escaped and is hiding
somewhere behind the prawn crackers...

And, worst of all, my dad has cleared his throat and is
about to SING!

La la la
Me me me

What I hadn't realised is that Sunday night is karaoke

night at The Red Emperor. Jeremy, the head waiter,

can't wait for my dad to start singing.

"Ladies and gentlemen,

please give a warm round

of applause for Mike Orsen!"

"Block your ears!" I shout.

"STICKY RIBS! STICKY RIBS!" shouts Otto.

Did I mention that Granny had snuck in her

pet parrot too? (Sneaking pets into

restaurants must be some sort of family thing.)

CRISPY SEAWEED!
CRISPY SEAWEED!

To take your mind off the singing here is...

BETH'S GUIDE TO ALL-YOU-CAN-EAT DINERS

I have noticed several TYPES of people at all-you-can-eat restaurants. Here are some of them...

The Architect

SMUG!

They can build towers of food that defy gravity.

The Dieter

SNEAKY! ⟶

They claim to only be eating vegetables (but watch them sneak 100 spring rolls under a lettuce leaf).

The Pick 'n' Mixer

They have to try EVERYTHING, often on the same plate at the same time.

What type are YOU?

GREEDY!

My dad's singing might be ruining *my* evening, but some

people seem to actually be enjoying it!

Dad sweating
and going red

"You must come back and sing again," says Jeremy. "In

fact I wouldn't be surprised if you weren't invited to the

REGIONAL KARAOKE competition."

Good
grief!

"That was FABULOUS!" gushes Richard (the way he

sucks up to my parents means he MUST be Mabel's

boyfriend – double yuck!). "I really think you could—"

Before he can finish, Richard lets out a huge

SQUEAL.

"My b-b-book bag – it, it moved!" he wails.

"Calculus books don't move," says Mabel, trying to

reassure him.

"My geometry set must be **HAUNTED!**,"

he says, trembling.

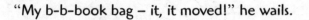

I would LOVE it if Richard's book bag was haunted –

There could be a *ghoul*

in his mini atlas...

A *goblin* in his

pencil case...

A *troll* in his

trigonometry book...

SUPER
advanced
trigonometry

But, of course, his bag isn't haunted – it's worse than that...

"Your **HORRID** pet! I should have guessed," says Mabel, as she realises what has been making the bag move. Scribbles!

"BETH," says Dad, as I realise I'm in

BIG TROUBLE...

Hey, why isn't the parrot getting told off?

Richard's **BULGING** book bag!

13

My dad starts to turn an alarming PURPLE colour.

"I, I, I thought that..." I stutter – but there really is no excuse for bringing a mouse to a Chinese restaurant, is there?

But then I am saved, rescued and relieved by a noise so horrendous my dad forgets all about Scribbles.

14

The sound that has saved me is the 'singing' of the next

karaoke singer. One after another they get up on stage,

and they are all **TERRIBLE**.

"I knew your father was
a great singer," says Mum,
who is smiling broadly.

"Yeah, those guys really need to work on their tone,"

chuckles Dad, who is in danger of getting a little bit

too smug.

butterflies of love... warble garble!

"Why don't you have a go, Beth?" asks my mum.

This is the worst suggestion Mum has made since she thought Clarissa Musgrove should come to our house for a sleepover (more about her later...).

Luckily, the judges have made a decision and someone's **won**.

Clarissa Musgrove - grrrrrr!

"Hey, it must be that lady at the next table," says Granny, because Jeremy is now heading in our direction with the TROPHY.

But he doesn't walk past our table. He stops right next to my dad. Because...

DAD. HAS. WON. THE. KARAOKE. COMPETITION.

NOOOOOOOOOOO!

Everybody claps and Otto screeches, "LOVELY TONSILS! LOVELY TONSILS!" Richard gets up and gives Dad a standing ovation.

Clap!

Clap!

Clap!

"After the regional competition you could go so much further," he says. "You could be the karaoke king!"

"And beyond that, a recording career!" says Mabel.

"Don't be so silly," pipes up Granny – but apart from me, no one is listening to her.

Dad's head is now so large I seriously wonder if he'll be able to get through the door of the restaurant, never mind into the car.

In the car, Mum makes an announcement.

"There was just so much excitement in there, what with your father and his singing, that I didn't get a chance to tell you—" she starts.

She then says something so

AWFUL

that I think that I might have

to hide under the car seat

with Scribbles

FOR THE NEXT 100 YEARS...

Me and
Scribbles

VERY OLD

Now, I know you're all anxious sausages, dying to find

out what the announcement was but, like meeting

Clarissa, that will have to wait – for a bit at least.

ANXIOUS SAUSAGES (Try saying *that* quickly!)

It's Monday morning and that means SCHOOL.

Wake up, Beth!

I might have forgotten all about the trip to the Red Emperor if Dad didn't insist on carrying his trophy with him everywhere.

I'm singin' in the bath...

"I'm not letting this bad boy out of my sight," he says, as he puts it next to his breakfast. As well as being an embarrassing singer, my dad quite often says things like 'bad boy'.

Bad boy!

Oh please!

Breakfast is even more of a disaster than usual because

Mum has to leave early as she is starting a new job today.

That means Dad is in charge...

AND IT'S A BIT OF A DISASTER!

I end up with a stack of sticky pancakes on my lap.

Bertie, my messy baby brother, ends up with sugar pops

in his hair.

And Mabel still manages to revise for her next exam.

Some facts about Mabel:

1. She is a **MEGA-NERD**

2. She doesn't like my drawings. After seeing a picture I doodled of myself she nicknamed me Badly Drawn Beth

3. In fact, she doesn't seem to like ANYTHING FUN!

YIKES!

As soon as I get changed – sticky maple syrup does not shift easily – I'm on my way to school. But when I get to the corner of my street, something is up.

"Where's Cordy?"
I mutter to myself.

It's not like her not to be here. Cordy is my best friend and normally I meet her every morning and we walk into school. Cordy is great and we always have the best chat – mostly about Dusk Light, our favourite film and book series.

She is ALWAYS here to meet me... something

HUGE

must have happened.

I'm out of here!

There are only three
possible solutions:

1. She has run away to join a troupe of travelling
TROLLS.

2. She has decided to grow a beard and **BECOME
A HERMIT** (and live in a distant cottage by the sea
somewhere).

3. She has finally become a vampire...and now lives at the top of a really tall tower, only emerging at night to feast on **BLOOD**!

With no sign of her, I walk on to school and assume that there is what my mum would describe as 'a perfectly sensible explanation' (which is probably true, even if it is a bit BORING).

When I finally get to school there is still no sign of
Cordy. I'm starting to get worried when I see a car
pull up.

"Beth! Come over here and help me," shouts a
familiar voice. It's Cordy, but there is something
different about her.

"Guess what! I broke my leg!" she says, as I help her out
of the car. "I've got 𝕔𝕣𝕦𝕥𝕔𝕙𝕖𝕤 and everything."

"What happened?" I ask as I help her into the playground. But she just looks at me **MYSTERIOUSLY**. "I knew I should never have ridden that griffin," she whispers.

Yeee! haaa!

Cordy is a bit wobbly on her feet, but apart from not being able to walk, having a cast is actually pretty **COOL**.

For starters, everyone wants to write something on it (I do a doodle of myself).

"Hey, that looks cool," says Cordy. (See, she doesn't think I look badly drawn!)

When you have a broken leg, everyone wants to help...

But every time someone asks Cordy how her leg got broken, she gives a different answer.

"I was on a space mission but tripped up in a black hole," she tells Anju.

Whoops!

"My pet sabre-tooth tiger knocked me over," she says to Zach.

I'm going to make her tell me what REALLY happened...but just then the school bell RINGS and we all have to go to class.

This is when having your leg in a cast is not quite so cool and I have to help Cordy in.

"Using crutches is soooo sloooow," she complains. "But it does give me the chance to tell you about the book I'm reading..."

We are both hugely into the

Dusk Light Saga –

a series all about

teenage werewolves.

But before Cordy can tell me more she stops, and her eyes seem to pop out.

"What's wrong, Cordy?" I ask.

Now, Cordy does tend to exaggerate things, but on this occasion she seems genuinely frightened. As Cordy gasps for air I quickly imagine the three most horrible sights you might see at school...

BETH'S GUIDE TO THE THREE MOST HORRIBLE SIGHTS YOU MIGHT SEE AT SCHOOL

1. A flesh-eating **ZOMBIE** gym teacher.

My hand just fell off...

2. The school dinner ladies **MAKING** stew (warning: look away if easily offended).

Marge, I found this behind the fridge...

3. The school janitor – Reginald Mavers – cleaning out a blocked **TOILET** with a stick.

This isn't going to be pretty...

But what Cordy has seen is actually WORSE –
because Cordy has seen...my mum!

That was the awful announcement my mum made at
the Red Emperor. She has a new job, the one she had
to leave early for, and it's as a temporary teacher at

MY SCHOOL!

NOT THE
POPPY-OUT
EYES AGAIN!

It's a great
look, trust me!

I had to plead with her to let me keep walking to
school with Cordy.

My mum is great, but think about it. Would you want your mum breathing down your neck all day long, checking up on you and generally being all over your life? NO!

"Hello Beth, hello Cordy. Poor you! What happened to your leg?" asks Mum, who is being all friendly.

But before Cordy can come up with another ridiculous reason, we are interrupted by the sound of a HORSE.

NEIGH HA HA HA NEIGH HA HA!

(OK, it's not a horse, it's Clarissa Musgrove laughing. She is finding the situation hilarious.)

"I can't believe your mum works at the school," she mutters under her breath as she walks past me. "I can't think of ANYTHING more embarrassing..."

Which tells you how silly Clarissa is – I can think of THOUSANDS of things that are more embarrassing, starting with her LAUGH, HER CHOICE OF RIDICULOUSLY EXPENSIVE HAND-BAGS and HER CONSTANT SHOWING OFF.

I am afraid I am going to have to introduce you to Clarissa.

Annoying 'I'm better than you' wave!

Absurdly fancy school bag

Clarissa is the really annoying girl in my class who looks down on everyone, especially Cordy and me.

Quick Clarissa Fact:

As well as being superior, snobby and generally annoying, her dad is my dad's BOSS and you can imagine how AWKWARD that gets, especially because Clarissa seems to think that makes her MY boss!*

Ah, yes, Orsen, I want a word with you. I just wanted to remind you that I'm the boss of you. Thank you, Orsen, you may go now.

ENORMOUS boss's chair

*It doesn't.

"I need to go to class," says my mum. "See you later." And with that – for now – she is gone. HUGE SIGH OF RELIEF.

PHEE-EWW!!!

At least my mum will not be teaching my class. When Cordy and I arrive, our teacher **Miss Primula*** is there, and in fine voice. In fact, she uses THAT voice – the one that sounds a bit like an angry android.

Hey, that's nothing like me!

(* pronounced PRIM-U–LA)

"Cordelia, you have a broken leg, you're allowed to be late," says Miss Primula with a scowl. "But you, Beth, what's your excuse?"

"Beth's MUMMY is working at the school," Clarissa pipes up, and the whole class guffaws.

Miss Primula's voice snaps out across the laughter.

She doesn't look that snappy...

"Thank you, Clarissa. Beth's mother is a very good teacher," she says. "We're very lucky to have her at our school. Now, I'm sure you're all dying to find out this term's theme..."

This is a very important moment.

Each term Miss Primula picks a THEME, something specific we will be working on. It could be anything from 'nature' or 'space' to 'spelling' or 'wildlife'. This will decide what I'll be spending most of my time at school (and quite a bit at home too) doing.

At the end of last term Cordy and I agreed we would be happy with most themes, as long as it wasn't...

CHEESE!

Cheese is most definitely MY department!

First Aid

(too much icky blood)

CRINGE!

It's only tomato sauce!

Driving A Bus

(we couldn't reach the pedals)

Why did we start on a hill! Help!

or Running The Country

(we are both FAR too busy to be prime minister).

The United Nations will have to wait. We haven't finished our shakes!

So we are relieved and delighted when Miss Primula tells us.

"This term's theme is READING," she declares. "And you will all be getting a free book!"

Tasty!

But, sadly, the books are not by the author Cordy and I would like – Jamilla Stenhouse, best-selling author of the **Dusk Light Saga** books.

She always wears chunky, funky jewellery!

"The books are by... Gerald Lassiter," announces Miss Primula.

"Gerald **WHO**?" I whisper to Cordy. But she hasn't heard of him either.

"He is the author of the *Roman Muse Chronicles*," says Miss Primula. "The exciting adventures of a Roman noble girl…"

Gerald Lassiter

EXCITING – ADVENTURES – ROMAN NOBLE GIRL…
Let me translate this for you:

DULL – DRY – EDUCATIONAL…
(AND NOT A TEENAGE WEREWOLF IN SIGHT).

I've lost my appetite.

This is a TOTAL READING **DISASTER!**

But there is no getting away from these books.
Miss Primula reaches into a box.

"Do swap them with each other when you have read yours," says Miss Primula, as she hands out the books. In front of me is my Gerald Lassiter book:

And Cordy's isn't much better.

"Enjoy! And, remember, I will be asking questions on your books," says Mrs Primula.

A few days later, the sun is shining and I'm doing what I like best – hanging out with Cordy. She is at my house so that we can read our books in the garden with a picnic.

First stop: the kitchen. We are going to have ice cream. But the freezer is empty.

Next, I suggest choccie biscuits. But these are all gone too.

"When Mum's at work full-time everything goes a bit wonky," I sigh.

Then I notice all the ingredients I need for a great snack.

43

I quickly make Cordy a cheese sandwich (as you can see, my sandwiches are SERIOUSLY big).

"I think you've broken your own world record," says Cordy, as she admires my mighty sandwich.

"It's actually going to be quite hard to get this through the garden door," I say as I carry our food through to the garden. Cordy follows on her crutches.

"I'd be happy to carry them, but my leg was broken by a stray STEGOSAURUS," says Cordy.

Why am I implicated?!?

I WILL find out what happened, I really will!

Once we're in the garden and we've finished the
sandwiches, it's finally time to read.

"These books are just soooo boring," says Cordy.
"Nothing happens."

"I actually like Roman stuff, but you're right," I agree.
"In my book, it takes four chapters for her just to run
a bath..."

Mummy, the
water is very
slow

"And in mine the big plot twist is she loses her purse on her way to market," sighs Cordy.

"Plot twist?" I say. "That doesn't sound much like a twist."

Alas! Where is my purse?

"Oh, the twist is she left it at home..." sighs Cordy again. We both groan.

"To think we could be reading the latest Dusk Light novel," says Cordy.

Dusk Light is 𝔟𝔯𝔦𝔩𝔩𝔦𝔞𝔫𝔱! In a typical American town lives a bunch of typical American teenagers. Except, wait for it – they are werewolves!

SPOOKY!

"Yeah, the books are where it all started," continues Cordy. "It all comes from the wonderful imagination of Jamilla Stenhouse..."

When you have seen all the movies, fallen for the lead actor (Bobby Gothick – swoon), have read the magazines, then you have GOT to read the books. They are sooooooooo good!

And now there is a new **Dusk Light** novel coming out!

As usual when it come to cool stuff, especially cool Dusk Light stuff, Cordy is the world expert.

MIDNIGHT
BOOK LAUNCH!

"So listen up," she says. "A little bird tells me there is going to be a midnight book launch at the shopping centre bookshop!"

This is **BIG** news.

little bird

"A little bird?" I say. Why would birds, even little ones, be talking to Cordy?

"It's an expression, Beth," harrumphs Cordy. "OK, it was my mum – she spotted it on the Dusk Light website. Jamilla Stenhouse herself will be there signing copies," she continues. "We have GOT to be there!"

DUSK LIGHT AUTHOR JAMILLA STENHOUSE IN **PERSON!!!**

This is going to require some serious planning. I'm not really in a position where I can say:

> "Hey, Mum, Dad. I'm off to the bookshop for a midnight signing. See you at 3a.m."

That's going to fly as high as a concrete kite. In other words: NO CHANCE. (I don't think concrete kites exist but if they did, they would be TERRIBLE at flying.)

But as Cordy and I start working on some schemes to get there, we are rudely interrupted by high-pitched squeals approaching the garden.

I think it's safe to say that high-pitched squeals are not a good thing. Ever.

"I don't think I've ever heard such a noise," says Cordy, covering her ears. "If I didn't have a broken leg I would run away... Curse the out-of-control Monster Truck that ran over it..."

But I already have a prime suspect...

No, it's not the neighbour's baby...

It's not a litter of lost kittens...

It's MABEL, giggling in a super-girly way!

Tee hee hee ooh hoo hoo hoo giggle squeal giggle

Mabel and her new 'best friend' Richard are heading straight towards us, carrying an enormous pile of school books.

For some reason, Mabel finds everything Richard says really funny.

"Could you two buzz off," says Mabel, shooing us away from the garden table.

"Yes, this is a bee-free table," adds Richard. Mabel finds this HILARIOUS and starts squeaking again.

How very dare you!

I was hoping Richard would have gone away by now, but he still seems to be hanging around.

So here are three RICHARD FACTS:

1. Although Richard is the same age as Mabel, he dresses like he is fifty!

2. Both his parents are doctors – no prizes for guessing what he wants to be when he grows up.

Say aaaaah!

3. His three favourite hobbies are: doing homework, doing more homework and doing even more homework with my sister.

I can't get enough of this.

VERY HARD MATHS

MATHS

They plonk their pile of maths and physics books on the

garden table – right where we are

reading.

"Gerald Lassiter's *Roman Muse*

Chronicles," says Richard,

noticing our books.

"*Lavinia and the Lukewarm Bath*," gushes Mabel. "We

read those books at school – they were excellent!"

"Hey, Mabel, remember the BRILLIANT

ending in the classic *Lavinia Reads a Poem*?"

Richard says.

"Oh, yes, it was AWESOME," gushes Mabel.

I suppose I should have guessed they would love those lame books.

"So, Lavinia is on stage in front of her sister and forgets her poem..." burbles Richard. "But she saves the day by – wait for it – singing!"

Richard is now ACTING OUT A BIT from the book...
IN FACT, HE IS SINGING—

HELP!

Do you have a spare amphora? Can you fill it up with water?

I block my ears I am seriously **FED UP** with singing this week – and I really don't believe that singing would save ANYTHING.

"Oh, Richard, that was wonderful!" says Mabel, but her smile turns upside down as she looks at us. "OK, seriously, guys – we need to do our physics and maths homework. Goodbye."

"We've got some, like, really important exams coming up," says Richard, in an annoyingly serious voice. "You guys wouldn't understand..."

What we have is a **STAND OFF**.

It's so tense!

"I think you'll find we were here first," I say.

"I think YOU'LL find I'm older and bigger than you, Badly Drawn Beth," replies Mabel.

Lalalalallaalalalalalal!!!

Mabel is interupted by another annoying noise. It's Dad, singing, and he needs the garden table too...

"It's the only place to dry all my hand-wash cardigans."

Baby Bertie is toddling behind Dad, carrying his karaoke trophy.

The garden is now far too busy and even though we were there first, Cordy and I decide to leave.

"Why do those two find everything so funny?" asks Cordy, as we hobble upstairs to the shelter of my bedroom.

But we have soon forgotten all about Mabel and Richard as we start plotting how to get to the Dusk Light Saga book launch.

Back at school, Miss Primula is teaching maths.

I quite like maths, but I don't mind being interrupted – because it's our head teacher, Ms Hailey, and she's dressed in a shiny Las Vegas-style dancers' outfit!

There are a couple of things you need to know about Ms Hailey – she is really

LOUD...

Helllooo!!!

And she loves to DRESS UP...

For 'Wildlife Week' she dressed up as a giraffe

It's me, Ms Hailey!

"Sorry to butt in, Miss Primula, but I couldn't hold this news back any longer!" she says in a LOUD voice.

"I'm going to every class to tell them..." Ms Hailey continues, before doing a little tap dance.

Clickety !

"Now, as you know, we have been joined by a new teacher," she starts.

This can only mean ONE PERSON. My tummy starts to do a little jiggle as I realise she's talking about my mum.

"We are delighted to have Mrs Orsen with us. But she is not here just to teach – she is here to

OVERSEE AND RUN

a special project!"

My mum! I am now panicking – Mum hasn't said anything to me about a special project.

What could it be?

Bricklaying?

Peeling potatoes?

Painting the moon?

Polishing elf boots?

Building a pyramid?

"The school is putting on a TALENT SHOW," says Ms Hailey. We all gasp – especially me!

"The talent show will be on the Saturday after the last day of term, in front of a huge audience of parents and guests. AND this is BIG, this is really BIG – there will be talent scouts looking for the next child star! It's going to be

HUGE!"

I'll do photos later!

Ms Hailey certainly has our attention now...

"And you, yes, all of you, will be the stars!" adds Ms Hailey as she dances her way out of the class, past a slightly confused-looking Miss Primula.

Shimmy! Shake!

There is a low, excited burble of noise as my class all talk about the announcement.

Let's take a quick look inside a few people's heads to see what they are thinking...

First of all, inside Clarissa's head. I'm pretty sure she is thinking: GREAT, this is an opportunity to show off – to buy some expensive outfits – to become a HUGE star – she is thinking FUN.

Inside my friend Anju's head...I bet she is thinking SUPER – she is thinking about making an awesome stage set – perhaps BUILDING some props – she is thinking FUN.

Inside Izzy's head – he is probably thinking AWESOME
– maybe I could do some football skills – it will be great
to perform in front of my family – he is thinking FUN.

What about my head? Well, inside my head are two
words, and two words only. MILD PANIC.

I'm not like my dad, or most of my class – I'm not sure I want everyone looking at me dancing or singing. I'm happy to watch other people, I'm just not convinced I have any talent, and certainly NOT any that I want anyone to see. And my mum in charge? **HELP!**

(I know you want to know what is going on inside Cordy's head – but she is just thinking:)

"Well, isn't this exciting?" says Miss Primula, as she quietens the room. "Now, I realise performing in front of an audience isn't for everyone, but it's really all about taking part... and I can assure everyone here that it's going to be fun."

I'm not so sure...

"Before we start to think about what we will do for the talent show," she continues, "let's get back to something EVEN MORE EXCITING..."

We all look at each other – what could this be?

"Maths!" says Miss Primula with a grin, and we all groan.

At home a few days later, and everyone is still talking about Mum and the talent show. Mum's really happy that her first few days went so well, but then she gets a bit serious.

She says, "As you know, I have new work commitments, what with all the extra hours I'm putting in at Beth's school…"

"I've been trying to do more at home," Dad says. "But things have got a bit chaotic…"

When I think about it, things HAVE been chaotic,
especially for Bertie...

Dad forgot to change
Bertie's outfit before
nursery and he went in
still dressed in his
PIRATE pyjamas.

When they went to the park
to play, Dad got confused
and took a watermelon
instead of a football.

And at bath time, he
mixed up the toothpaste
and the shampoo.

"We've decided the Orsen family will need a new
childminder," Mum declares.

We have had a number of childminders over the years, but for some reason NONE of them have lasted too long.

"It's really important that this works out," says my father in a serious voice.

"Yes, I don't want any repeat of some of the nonsense we've had in the past," adds Mum.

When my mum says 'NONSENSE', I think she is actually referring to some of the great times we had with past childminders.

There was the time when Scribbles decided to take up residence in a childminder's handbag...

I do NOT do rodents!

The next childminder
was getting on just fine
until I needed to use
her hat as a mop...

And who could
forget when Mabel
'accidentally' swapped
the sugar for chilli powder...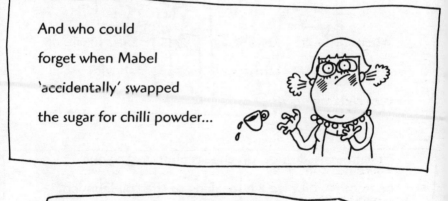

It was an honest mistake!

Two days later, my parents are interviewing childminders and Mabel, Bertie and I have been put under room arrest.

Mum! Dad! You really don't need to post a house troll outside my door!

BETH'S ROOM

"That means do not, on any account, leave your bedrooms whilst we are speaking to the childminders," declares Dad.

I'm not quite sure what he is expecting us to do that will be so terrible, but we all reluctantly go to our rooms.

In my room I have got **TWO** options.

I either think up ideas
for the talent show – yuck!

Or

I read my Gerald Lassiter
book – double yuck
with a polished extra
yuck on the side.

Of course, what I really want to know is what is going
on downstairs.

It's on days like
this I wish I could
strap a camera to
Scribbles's back.

He would become
SPY MOUSE!

He could sneak down

into the kitchen using

SECRET PASSAGES.

He would then creep along the top of the cupboard

and hide between the jam and the honey pot.

This would give him a perfect viewpoint to watch the

interviews and beam back live camera footage...

Which I would watch from the comfort of a huge **VILLAIN** chair stroking my VILLAIN's cat in my VILLAIN's lair...

Sadly, strapping cameras to the backs of mice – even one as clever as Scribbles – is NOT a good idea. Not only that, but I don't have a villain's cat or lair – in fact, I'm not even a villain.

So, I eventually pick up my book... but my mind keeps wandering. Although every childminder is different, there are a few types...

Beth's Guide to Childminders

1. The Old Battleaxe – has been a childminder

for 100 years for over 1000 kids and they

were ALL better behaved

than me...

Shhhhh!

2. The Cool Guy –

likes to think we are

FRIENDS (YUCK!)

and that he is not looking

after us but we are

'hanging out'.

I don't think so.

Let's start a band!

3. The Dippy Hippy –

look, I like making things, but this childminder wants to make stuff ALL THE TIME. And they put BEANS in everything.

If my parents had asked me, I would have told them that my perfect childminder would be:

This little bean is, like, so totally awesome that is has, like, the same protein as a whale! Awesome! Let's make a den! Like, NOW!

Part kids' entertainer... part ice-cream super chef...

And part magician...

But I don't suppose any of them are like that.

The next day, in class, I'm filling Cordy in on the latest news from home and Miss Primula spots me whispering. I know what comes next – the scary voice!

"BETH..." starts Miss Primula.

Just then there's a knock and the classroom door opens...

It isn't an ogre with bad teeth, demanding to KISS me...

Or the Reading Police
demanding to
know why I haven't finished
my Lavinia book yet...

You guessed it, it's my MUM!

"Mrs Orsen!" exclaims Miss
Primula, like my mum is her
long-lost friend. "Class, you will be pleased to hear that
you'll be getting a break from normal lessons. For the
next lesson, I am handing over to Mrs Orsen as it will be
all about the talent show..."

"Thank you, Miss Primula," says Mum, before turning to
my class.

Mum now tells us exactly what is going to happen
between now and the end of term. No wonder she has
been busy. She puts up a list on the whiteboard:

TALENT SHOW – HOW IT IS GOING TO WORK:

1. First of all, you will be put into groups.

2. You will work out WHAT you want to perform together, who is going to write it, direct it, make the costumes, etc.

3. Each group will have a five-minute slot to entertain the crowd.

4. You can sing a song, perform a dance, do a comedy routine or anything else you can think of to show off your talents.

This already looks FAR TOO COMPLICATED, but there is no escaping the fact the talent show is going to happen...

"OK, so let's get started," says my mum.

"A lot of this is going to be about
TEAMWORK."

She then forms us into groups.
I am grateful to be with Cordy
(who's still on crutches) and Izzy.

Mum's team
work gesture

But being put into teams is the easy bit.

"To get things started, let's just get together and bounce
a few ideas around," says Mum.

For the rest of the class we get to 'bounce ideas around'
– although I would happily bounce them out of the
classroom window and bounce away...

We sit in circles to discuss what we might do. In
my group there is a mad mixture of **TERROR** and
EXCITEMENT.

81

After ten minutes we have come up with... a big, enormous

NOTHING!

(OK, one thing, we decided to call ourselves 'Team Howler' but that's it!)

This talent-show business is not going to be easy. But fortunately Mum gives us a break – for now.

"Why don't you all have a think about it over the next couple of weeks?" she suggests as the school bell rings.

Clarissa and her friends – the yucky Desiree Fogle and the creepy Josh Wyndham – have been whispering and plotting all lesson, and they decide to work through break time.

We are going to have to come up with something REALLY GOOD to beat them...

That Saturday, Mum and Dad introduce us to our new childminder, Sonia.

She is friendly...

It's strange, but I like the Dusk Light Saga too!

Then she is funny:

I can do all kinds of animal impressions - bark, woof, meow!

Bark!   Woof!   Meow!

And finally she is kind...

When I'm not making your favourite meals, maybe I can help out with your homework?

This all makes me really, really **SUSPICIOUS**.

Sonia is TOO PERFECT. Something HAS to be going on.

I SMELL A RAT

Just then Cordy arrives and she gets to meet Sonia too. Like me, she is not falling for it.

"Classic vampire," says Cordy, as she hops up the stairs to my room. "I've seen that type before. The smiling face, the nice clothes, the being friendly to younger brothers..."

"All a bit too good to be true," I agree, although I think that Cordy's theory may be a bit extreme. After all, vampires aren't known for making delicious home-made garlic bread. In any case, we decide to keep a close eye on Sonia.

This will start with the tea that Sonia has made for us.

Cordy and I are taking secret notes...

"Don't miss anything," I whisper to Cordy, as she fills her

plate with our favourite sausages and chips.

"And don't trust anything," Cordy hisses at me, as I fill

my plate with my favourite pancakes for pudding. "This

is clearly a set up!"

Now, apart from tea being **SUSPICIOUSLY**

amazing, we have come up with nothing. It is only later

that evening, when my dad is discussing Sonia with my

mum, that I hear a vital bit of information.

"Sonia has been brilliant," gushes Mum. "Not only is her impression of a giraffe HILARIOUS, but the kids all seem to really like her..."

"I knew she would be great," says my dad (and this next bit is the vital bit of information). "She used to work for the Musgroves... apparently Clarissa really liked her."

SONIA IS A MUSGROVE SPY!

Clarissa must have sent her to spy on me to find out what I'm planning for the school talent show.

But before I can do anything I need PROOF. Cordy and I are watching and we will miss NOTHING!

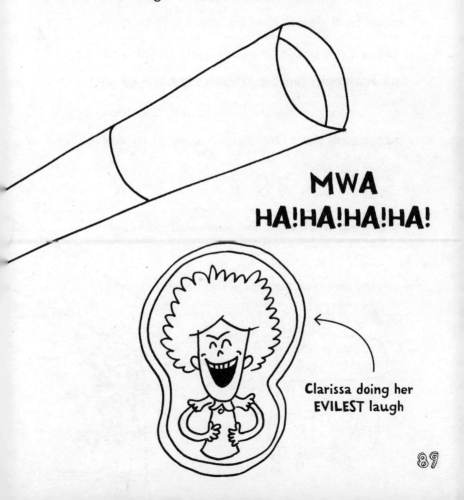

MWA HA!HA!HA!HA!

Clarissa doing her EVILEST laugh

89

Meanwhile, we have other important work to do — we have to persuade our parents that we can be allowed to go to the Dusk Light book launch. It doesn't sound hard — but the launch is at MIDNIGHT and involves queuing for HOURS. But if we want to get the new Dusk Light novel (and we do) then we HAVE to be there.

It's in a week's time, so I need to get to work.

In the past, there have been two ways I have asked for things like this.

I have either shouted and screamed and begged...

OR shouted and screamed and begged even LOUDER.

Not a pretty sight, I agree.

But recently, neither of these approaches have worked
so I need to think up a third way.

And when I hear that Cordy's mum has already agreed,
(as Cordy said, "How could she say no to someone
whose leg was broken by a falling meteorite?") the
pressure is now on me.

Oh dear!

I try hopping around and making "ouch" noises, but
I soon realise that to get sympathy for a broken leg you
must actually HAVE a **broken leg**...

I decide on a brand-new approach – I swap shouting, screaming and begging for squirming, pleading and grovelling (which is a bit like my old approach but less noisy).

PLEASE, PLEASE, PLEASE, PLEASE, PLEASE...

It's not big and it's not clever – but my parents finally agree. I CAN GO!

But there are some serious conditions:

"First of all you've got to finish your reading book," says Dad.

"*Lavinia and her Lukewarm Bath.* Check!" I say.

"Then you've really **GOT** to write your act for the talent show," says Mum. "Clarissa's group have already got their whole act sorted."

"I will write, script and choreograph like my life depends on it," I say.
"I already have lots of ideas."

Izzy! More jazz hands!

We do, but they're mainly ideas about how to run away from the talent show really fast.

"And finally, you've got to be nice to Sonia," says my dad.

Is it me or are these conditions getting tougher?

"I will be sweet and lovely and gorgeous," I reply.

I will be nice to her but I will still be keeping
A VERY CLOSE EYE ON HER.

In the next talent show lesson, Mum gives me an ENCOURAGING GRIN. But it's no good – my group is seriously behind.

Everyone is in their teams, practising. In one corner Anju and her group are coordinating their roller-skate routine; in another, Zach and his friends are tuning up their ukuleles; and Clarissa's team is wearing tutus and doing weird vocal singing exercises.

Cordy, Izzy and I are starting to panic.

"The other teams have got their talents all sorted," says Izzy. "They all look so professional."

"OK, guys," says my mum. "Would anyone here like to show us what they have got so far? And remember that you have to wave an arm in the air when you finish so the next group knows it's their turn to go onstage."

No prizes for guessing who CAN'T WAIT to show us their entry. **TEAM TUTU.**

Clarissa and her friends Desiree and Josh are soon centre stage. But before they start, Clarissa says something that makes my knees go wobbly (and not in a good way).

"We go to," says Clarissa, "Stagecraft School..."

Let me tell you all about Stagecraft School.

Stagecraft School is a weekly Saturday morning class where you learn how to sing, act and dance...

Saturday morning!
I could be doing lots
of things: snoozing,
dozing, napping,
grabbing 40 winks,
visiting the Land of Nod...

And last year, for some reason, my mum and dad thought it would be a good idea to sign me up.

When we got there I had a terrible time. For starters,
the man in charge, Germane DeFoot, was one of those
annoyingly enthusiastic guys.

But no matter what they tried to teach me, I just wasn't
very good. My singing was bad, my acting was *really* bad
and my dancing was terrible.

And who should be there in every class? Clarissa, that's who! And she was loving it!

But as if that wasn't bad enough, there was even worse to come.

As you will know by now, I quite often take my pet mouse Scribbles with me to places where you wouldn't really expect to find a mouse.

So you won't be surprised that one Saturday I took Scribbles to Stagecraft School. And I would have got away with it, if Germane DeFoot hadn't been allergic to animals...

EEEEEEEEEEEEEEK!

And when I say ALLERGIC, I mean he sneezed so loudly the furniture shook. When he discovered Scribbles I was politely asked to leave.

(I was BANNED FOR LIFE.)

Secretly pleased!

But Clarissa and her friends never stopped going, which means right now is the moment they have been waiting for...

"We've really struggled to pick ONE of our skills to showcase," Clarissa gloats.

My mum is doing that twitchy eyebrow thing that she does when she's annoyed, but she covers it up with her calm teacher voice.

"We can't wait to see what you've got," says my mum.

"Well, our actual act is TOP SECRET," Clarissa says, with a grin that makes her look like she is auditioning for a toothpaste commercial. "In fact, my parents hired Germane DeFoot himself to assist," she says, smugly.

Surely this is illegal???

"Why don't you just give us a little sample?" Mum suggests, her calm voice getting stretched.

THE HORROR!

Now we have to all sit down to watch Clarissa. And she is loving the attention.

STOP! That face is so smugnificently smug that it is a danger to public health. You must NOT see it!

They start their act. It seems to be a mixture of the Dance of the Sugar Plum Fairy and a girl band. They are wearing tutus and twirling as they sing a pop song...

A pop song so catchy that I CANNOT get it out of my head!

Team Tutu is go! Team Tutu is go! We know that we'll make it - we've got a great show! Oh, yeah!

It's awful but SO CATCHY, and the crowd seems to be liking it.

"Well done, Clarissa, that was marvellous," beams my mum.

Cordy, Izzy and I look at each other in despair. The pressure really, REALLY is on now!

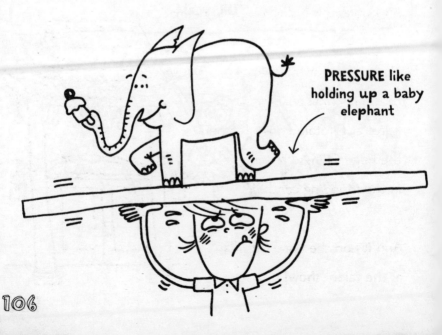

PRESSURE like holding up a baby elephant

I'm in the kitchen at home a few days later and a terrible noise is coming from upstairs. Dad is practising his karaoke. It is driving everyone mad

He has just got his invitation to the regional championships – live at Captain Fong's Kitchen, the huge Chinese restaurant in the shopping centre.

And it's on the same Saturday as the talent show!

The next day Cordy and I call an EMERGENCY
TEAM HOWLER MEETING at my house.
Izzy grumbles but agrees to come round after football
practice.

After the last session we are in a panic. We have got to
write a brilliant routine!

Mum is a bit suspicious because all my talent show
group is here.

Izzy's here!
Team Howler
is GO!

Izzy's never been to my house before — well, not since my disastrous fourth birthday party and the whole class was invited. Let's just say jelly, bouncy castles and mice don't mix.

"You *have* written your routine, haven't you?" Mum says, as I usher everyone upstairs. Cordy can still only hop with her broken leg, but I pretend not to hear until Cordy's inside my room and I can shut the door.

But even when we're stuck in my room with no distractions, the planning is still going badly. Suddenly, my room feels like a terrible place to be. Right now I would rather we were:

We could make a cocoboat?!?

A. On a desert island discussing how to escape using our last bunch of coconuts

B: Playing dominoes with a giant squid

or even

C: Locked in a Chinese restaurant listening to my dad singing.*

* OK, maybe not that...

"Come on, guys," says Cordy. "There must be something we can do. Clarissa has already written her entry."

We're just about to have a breakthrough when there's a knock at the door. It's Sonia.

"How are you getting on?" she asks. "I've brought you milk and biscuits..."

Milk and biscuits? Microphones and hidden cameras, more like. I am still convinced she is spying on us.

'Jammy Custard Crumbly'? I don't think so!

But I'm on to her and, to be on the safe side, I make sure no one says anything about our act until we've eaten ALL THE BISCUITS and drunk ALL THE MILK.

Finally we are alone. And very full. But we are running out of time and with Clarissa getting professional help, we need to do something SPECTACULAR.*

A volcano would be good...

*Although right now we would settle for quite good.

Cordy suggests we write a dark, spooky song. But our version of 'The Wheels on the Vampire Bus' is dreadful...
"I think our singing is making the neighbourhood cats run away," says Izzy, looking out of the window.

I suggest that we do a dance – but it turns out we have about as much rhythm as a STONE.

"I've seen tables with better moves," says Cordy.

Finally we try Izzy's 'comedy scene'.

This involves a goalkeeper (played by Cordy) who has left her glasses at home. I'm the referee who gives a penalty when Izzy is tripped up in the box.

"This is about as funny as a dead leg," admits Izzy, forgetting about Cordy's broken leg. Cordy just gives him an evil stare.

So far we have,

"We're going to have to get some inspiration from somewhere," says Cordy.

And there's something MEGA EXCITING happening this weekend which might give us the chance to find it...

This weekend it's finally the release of the latest Dusk Light novel!

This is MAJOR excitement. It's going to involve a lot of queuing and not much sleep BUT I get to hang out with my best friend (just the two of us — no parents or older sisters) and I get to buy the new book. Awesome!

THAT IS HAPPY!

As we load the car to head to the book shop at the shopping centre we check we have everything we need:

List

(a) Sleeping bags

(b) 15 layers of clothing

(c) Picnic for midnight snack made by Sonia so probably booby-trapped

(d) Flask of hot soup

We now set off in the car and for once my dad has
promised NOT TO SING.

When we get there the rest of the shopping centre is
closing for the night, but there are lots of people
milling around the bookshop.

"Look at the crowd!" I gasp.

There is an amazing buzz and we can hardly believe we
are here. The bookshop windows are filled with Dusk

Light posters. There are people in Dusk Light T-shirts all around us. The queue has already formed, with some fans in deckchairs, and others in tents. It's like a Dusk Light festival, and Cordy and I are right there!

"We need to get into position as soon as possible," says Cordy, who barges past some shoppers to take a spot. "Excuse me, please! My leg was broken by a

 GIANT COCKROACH."

Not guilty!

There is a special rope-barrier marking out the queue so we know where to go.

"This is so exciting!" I say, as we put down our sleeping bags.

"It's going to be great!" says Cordy.

"Is there a toilet nearby?" says my dad.

MY DAD. He did not drop us off and drive away.

Yes, at the last minute my dad has decided he needs to stay to "keep an eye on us".

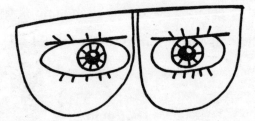

But we are determined **NOT** to let him ruin our fun.

Cordy and I quickly come up with a plan.

"The best thing would be for him to fall asleep," whispers Cordy.

Zzzzzz

We make sure he has the most comfortable position.
He has brought a TENT and lots of outdoor gadgets. We
help him set up his tent in the queue and check he is
nice and warm.

"I'm so warm and cosy in my camping cardigan," he says
with a yawn. In no time he is snoring away...

Cordy and I can now enjoy
being at the coolest
place in town.

Yay!

HAPPY
HAPPY!
JOY JOY!

We are surrounded by fellow Dusk Light fans. Some of them are dressed in costumes (I wish Cordy was still taking her Swamp Monster mask everywhere); some of them have memorabilia and posters to be signed. We are so close to the bookshop we can almost touch the new book.

This is GREAT!

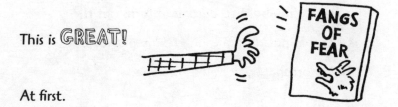

At first.

The trouble is, we now have to wait... and wait... AND WAIT – and I am not very good at waiting.

Cordy is even WORSE at waiting than I am.
"I'm SO bored!" she says.

"But, we've only been here for seven minutes," I tell her.

"The bookshop doesn't open for another five hours!"

5 HOURS IS A WHOPPING 300 MINUTES!!!!!

"FIVE HOURS!" gasps Cordy. "How are we going to last for FIVE HOURS!"

Just when we're about to despair, it turns out the bookshop has put on some entertainment for the crowd. Unfortunately, it's all a bit lame.

This is not helping the time to pass, but has woken up my dad.

"Cool, groovy and seriously hip sounds!" says Dad. He seems to be the only person here who is into the one-man band.

"Do you think he would let me sing backing vocals?" asks Dad. But I shoot him a stare that would take paint off a wall and I think he gets the message.

Instead, he pours out the soup Mum made us bring.

This is actually a great idea because it is getting **COLD**.
And if there is one thing worse than being **BORED**, it's
being cold and bored.

After our warm soup we decide to try and get a bit of
sleep in our official DUSK LIGHT sleeping bags.

"Whatever happens, Beth – no actual sleeping!" yawns
Cordy as we lie down. "We don't want to lose
our place in the queue."

"Certainly not," I say. "Do you... really... think...."

Cordy and I are waiting in the queue when a limousine

pulls up alongside us...

We are invited into the car (even my dad gets to come),

and driven to an airport...

Here we are flown to a private island – an island that belongs to Jamilla Stenhouse, the author and creator of the Dusk Light Saga...

We hang out on the island, eating great food, swimming in the pool and occasionally coming up with story ideas for new Dusk Light novels...

I LOVE that plotline, Beth!

Then we all go for a horse ride, but one of the horses there is laughing at us... because it's all a DREAM!

DISASTER!

We both fell asleep! And the horse is Clarissa, LAUGHING at us.

"Neighhahahhahahah!" she cackles. "Well, if it isn't Sleeping Beauty, her friend and Daddy!"

"What's going on?" says Cordy, who has woken up with a start. My dad is next to me, his mouth wide open as he snores.

Over Clarissa's shoulder we can see the bookshop is closing. We have slept through the entire book launch!

We have missed

EVERYTHING!

"I just bought the last copy of this silly little book," Clarissa says with a laugh.

"But you don't even like the Dusk Light Saga!" I say.

Clarissa actually hates the books, but has bought **THE LAST COPY** as a present for her brother Keffin.

And gloatingly, smugly – very Clarissary – she shows us Jamilla Stenhouse's signature on the book's title page (grrrrr!!!).

It's a total **DISASTER**!

Monday at school is not a good day.

For starters, me and Cordy are exhausted from our pointless trip to the bookshop.

Even though we have searched all over town, we can't find a copy of the book anywhere.

They DO NOT look happy!

But worse is to come, because today is the day my mum is putting together the list of acts for the talent show and we STILL don't have anything!

"I'm sorry, guys," says Mum, "but I'm going to have to assign you something. How about...'Goldilocks and the Three Bears'?"

Cordy, Izzy and I groan. "I'm sure you know the story," Mum continues. "Why don't you remind us, Beth."

The whole class laughs. Of course I know the story – it's a fairy tale aimed at LITTLE KIDDIES.

Hello, I'm Goldilocks and I LOVE porridge!

"Oh, yes – Goldilocks is an alien who lands on a planet made of porridge," I start... But as soon as Mum's eyebrow twitches, I quickly give the real story.

"Goldilocks is a naughty girl who breaks into the three bears' house, eats all their porridge, sits in their chairs, sleeps in their beds and complains about everything. The bears come home to find her asleep in one of the beds. But she runs away and doesn't even get punished. Oh, yes, and she has lots of curly blonde hair..."

"You will perform a five-minute sketch based on 'Goldilocks and the Three Bears'," says Mum. "A sketch is a short comedy routine. Now, everyone in your groups and get to work!"

It is then that I have my brainwave!

Wooo hooo!

"Wait a second," I say. "We could give it a Dusk Light twist."

"That's a great idea," says Cordy.

"What's Dusk Light?" says Izzy, who is so into football he doesn't really know about anything else that is going on.

But Cordy and I have it sorted. Our talent show entry will be a short sketch called, 'Goldilocks and the Three Werewolves!'

We are now officially in business, cooking, rocking, rolling and any number of other words that mean that things are going well.

First of all we need to write the outline of the scene... We quickly cast ourselves as the three werewolves; I will also double-up as Goldilocks (this will require a quick costume change and a huge blonde wig).

This could actually work!

Yes, that IS me!

I have taken on the role of writer. My job is to make the fairy tale sound as much like Dusk Light as possible. Cordy is going to direct – and she is making it as creepy and spooky as she can.

Finally, Izzy is going to be our lead actor, Mr Werewolf (he doesn't have the swoon factor of Bobby Gothick, but his growly voice is actually quite good).

Mum, who is moving from group to group, comes to see how we are getting on. And we give her a sneak peek (but make sure the rest of the class can't hear us):

GOLDILOCKS AND THE THREE WEREWOLVES!

The scene is set – the three werewolves' house has been visited...

Me, Cordy and Izzy (we'll all be dressed as werewolves) have some questions we need answered. First up, it's Izzy as Mr Werewolf:

This is way outta line! Who has been sitting in our DOG BASKETS?

Then we'll go to the KITCHEN, and it's now my line as
Baby Werewolf.

This is un-cool. Who has been eating our DOG FOOD???

And, finally, when we make a terrible discovery, Cordy
asks the question as Mrs Werewolf...

Dancing dog biscuits! Who has been sleeping in our KENNELS???

I'll then make a quick switch from being Baby Werewolf into Goldilocks (I definitely need a wig) and flee the house. Huge laughs. Massive applause. Talent spotter signs us up right then! (Well, maybe...)

"It's inspired by the latest Dusk Light novel," I declare.

"And what is that about?" Mum asks.

"We have no idea," replies Cordy. "We slept through the book launch, remember?"

"But this *could* be in it," I say.

Mum seems to be really excited by our idea and she moves on to the next group muttering words like "inspiring", "fascinating" and "can't wait to see what you do with it..."

In fact, the whole class is taking notice — and I am DELIGHTED to see that Clarissa is clearly not happy. She has a massive sulky frown and her nostrils are twitching.

NOT A PRETTY SIGHT!

"I think Clarissa can smell the competition," I chuckle to Cordy.

"She had better get used to that smell — because this sketch is going to be the biggest stink at the talent show," says Cordy.

Delightfully whiffy!

I think she means 'stink' in a good way...

Sadly, rehearsals have to stop – yes, sadly, because we are now really enjoying them.

"Everyone back to your places," says Mum. "Rehearsals are over for today – next, I suggest you get your costumes ready for the show."

"We need to do our own costumes!" says Cordy. "I'd forgotten about that."

I have a SECRET COSTUME-MAKING WEAPON, but before I can explain, our class teacher is back and Miss Primula has given me THE LOOK, backed up by THE VOICE!

The Look

The Voice

I had almost forgotten – this term's theme is reading.

Miss Primula had certainly not forgotten!

"So, I trust you have all been doing your reading," says Miss Primula. "Who would like to tell me a bit about their book?"

The usual hands shoot up. In fact it would appear that the only people who have not yet read their books are me and Cordy!

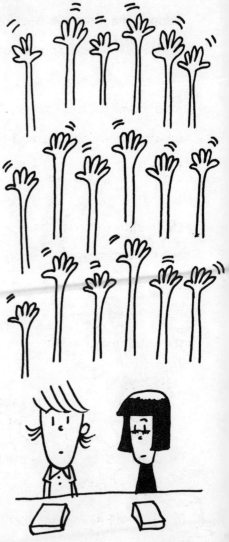

"How about you, Beth – what did you think of your book? You're reading *Lavinia and the Lukewarm Bath*, aren't you?" asks Miss Primula.

I have one of those moments when I want a giant lift
to appear and sweep me away. But when that doesn't
happen, I confess I haven't read it and
PROMISE to read it as soon as I can.

Back home, in the kitchen, Dad is
looking annoyingly pleased with
himself.

He has got that 'cat that
got the cream' look so badly
that I wouldn't be surprised if
he sprouted ears and a tail and
started drinking milk from a bowl.

145

"Great news!" he says. "I hope you're all sitting down..."

"Get a move on, Dad," says Mabel. "I have more revising to do."

"Well, you'll need to take a break tomorrow," he continues, "because I have a Sunday treat for us!"

Our ideas of a 'Sunday treat' are all very different. Mabel's idea of a treat is a visit from Richard, her icky revision buddy, and a day alphabetising her books and making colour-coded study plans.

Mine is a hang-out session with Cordy, with a triple layer fudge-strawberry knickerbockerglory...

I'll get a ladder and two big spoons!!!

"I know you're busy!" Dad says as we complain, "but on Sunday we are going to the golf club!" Dad beams. "We've been invited to Donny Musgrove's birthday party and – wait for it..."

(While we're waiting for it, I should remind you that Donny Musgrove is not only Clarissa's dad, he is also my dad's boss.)

"I will be singing him a special birthday ballad!" he says. Just then Sonia arrives, with a lasagne.

Oooh! Cheesy topping!

"And it was all thanks to Sonia," adds my mum. "She mentioned to Muriel Musgrove that your dad was keen to practise his singing and, before you know it, we were invited!"

This is the last straw – Sonia is definitely in cahoots with the Musgroves. This must be a trap!

We are being set up and somehow Sonia is going to find out all about my sketch and tell Clarissa. I will be super-extra-mega vigilant.

Me being beady-eyed and not missing a thing!

I suddenly need to pack all my weekend plans into Saturday. With some extra speed-reading skill, I finally finish my Lavinia book.

Weird speed-reading eyeballs!

It might not be Dusk Light but it's not that bad.

I can now let Izzy and Cordy into my TOP SECRET COSTUME WEAPON... my granny!

My granny used to work in the costume department for the movies. SHE is my secret costume-making weapon!

"This is great," says Cordy as we arrive at Granny's.
"Who else is going to have a professional dressmaker?"

"Clarissa?" suggests Izzy, who has met us there.
He's probably right, but we decide not to think
about that too much right now.

"Come in, come in!" says Granny.

Just as I hoped, she is
delighted to be involved.
"Now, before we do any
costumes, I have a very
serious question to ask you."

Both Cordy and Izzy look a bit
concerned. But I know what's
coming next.

"Who would like... a slice of cake?" beams Granny.

151

We are soon all sitting around the kitchen table eating **HUGE** slices of cake.

"I call it the Chocolate and Caramel Double or Quits cake," says Granny.

"Double or Quits cake?" asks Izzy, with his mouth full.

"Yes, it's got DOUBLE of everything!" cackles Granny.
"And I know no one will quit eating it!"

Everyone laughs as they tuck in.
Everything is going well.
Even Otto is behaving
himself (at first anyway).

I should introduce you
to Otto properly – he is
Granny's pet parrot.

He can be a bit moody
and often shouts out
random things.

Today he is on best behaviour
until he notices Izzy's hat.

In fact, he seems to quickly develop a hatred of Izzy's hat and soon goes on the attack, dive-bombing it and screeching rude things.

Mucky barnet!

Eventually Izzy takes his hat off.

After cake, we are all ushered into Granny's sewing room. I haven't been in there for ages and I forgot just how ACE it is.

Granny made costumes for lots of movies and on every wall are pictures of old film stars (most of whom I've never heard of).

People like:

Swedish starlet Gertrude Svenn,

Comedy star Hugo France,

And hunky action hero Arnweld Schwartzkapf

I can see that Izzy and Cordy are impressed.

"Have you met Bobby Gothick?" asks Cordy.

"He's after my time," replies Granny. "But I have made werewolf outfits before, for a film called *Day of The Hounds.*"

"That sounds fun," says Izzy, who is now mostly relieved to be away from Otto.

"Fun?" snaps Granny. "It was a HORROR film. In it, the main star turns into a werewolf who is hunted by the villagers. The only way he escapes is by pretending to be a sheep. So I have plenty of experience making hairy outfits. Now, let's measure you up," says Granny.

She gets out an ancient-looking tape measure. "And you'll be needing a wig, Goldilocks."

In no time she has all of our measurements down and is rummaging through piles of old material.

"How long do you think it will take to make the costumes?" I ask, as she starts to sew.

"A couple of days," she replies. "I'll call your mum when they're ready."

And so we leave, but Izzy has to go without his hat – Otto has tried to make a nest in it!

The next day is Sunday and we have the big family trip to the golf club. Of course my parents are super excited.

"If this goes well then Donny might ask me to play a round of golf with him," says my dad. "If I could only play a one-on-one round of golf with Mr Musgrove, I would be able to ask for that promotion."

When we arrive there is a huge banner that says:

HAPPY BIRTHDAY MR MUSGROVE.

There are friends, family and, of course, Clarissa in FULL GOLF GEAR. This involves lots of brightly coloured clothes. Although of course she thinks she looks amazing!

Clarissa must have read my GUIDE TO GOLF CLOTHES.

BETH'S GUIDE TO GOLF CLOTHES

1. No two items of clothing should ever match.

2. No colour is too loud. In fact, colours you have never even heard of like PLUM, CERISE and VERMILLION are all good.

And

3. If in doubt, wear TARTAN. This works especially well on hats (and all golf hats must look silly).

"Hello everyone!" beams Muriel Musgrove. "After some fun on the golf course, we are going to have a lovely birthday tea!"

But I've seen something that's chilled me to the bone.

SONIA IS THERE, 'HELPING OUT' THE MUSGROVES.

But before I can investigate I am now expected to play golf. Against Clarissa.

Apart from one round of crazy golf on holiday I have never played golf before. It's a total disaster!

First of all, I hit a ball right into the back of Mr Musgrove's head!

THWACK!
THUNK!

Ooof!

Then I let go of my golf club and it ends up in a pond.

The final disaster is when Bertie lets off the handbrake on my golf buggy...

But when we gather in the club room Mr Musgrove

seems surprisingly happy.

"I have never laughed so much on
a golf course!" he beams. "What
a pleasure it has been to have
been joined by my lovely
member of staff, Mr
Orsen, and his family..."

At that very moment my dad appears to

sing the birthday ballad. He's carrying our present for

Mr Musgrove – the Golfing Pro Putt-a-Tron 3000,

a special gadget for practising golf in the office!

This is Dad's big moment. My mum is beaming with pride. Richard and Mabel are holding hands. Eurk! (I should have guessed Richard would be here – his parents are members of the golf club. Groan!)

Even Clarissa is smiling – but then everything goes into slow motion...

Just as Dad starts to sing, the golf ball rolls off the Putt-a-Tron 3000 and my dad slips on it. As he falls he hits a note so HIGH that glasses shatter and the cutlery starts to clatter...

Mr Musgrove puts his hands over his ears, but as he does so, he trips on the golf ball too – and topples into the table where his huge chocolate birthday cake is...

I gasp. My mum gasps. Clarissa Musgrove gasps.
Mr Musgrove is now wearing his birthday cake like some kind of weird hat. It is not a good look.

SPLAT!!!

Even by my family's standards, this is a total

CATASTROPHE.

"If this is some sort of practical joke, I'm not laughing,"
says Donny. "Golf is over for today..."

As we drive home the car is quiet. My dad doesn't even
want to sing along to the radio.

"What a terrible accident," says my mum.
"What are the chances of that?" mutters Dad. "I'd
rehearsed that walk a million times..."

165

When I tell Cordy what happened the next day at school we are certain – this was no accident.

"A golf ball? Really?!?" says Cordy. "Sonia MUST have been behind it. It was a set up!"

"My thoughts exactly," I say.

But before I can finally expose Sonia, there is the last talent show rehearsal.

It's a total turnaround! Our rehearsal goes great:

ROAR!!!

We get every line spot on... Izzy howls in all the right places and I even remember to wave my arm to signal for Clarissa and Team Tutu to come on when we're finished.

"I think you guys could be the dark horses of this talent show," says Mum. "I think the talent spotter may well be interested in you!"

(Which *is* very kind, but she *is* my mum!)

Have you ever had one of those weekends where there is just a little, ickle bit too much going on?

By which I mean there *is* WAY, HUGELY, RIDICULOUSLY TOO MUCH GOING ON?

I've had one of those weekends: I once had to eat *this* much cheese!

Well, this is going to be one of those weekends. First of
all it's the KARAOKE REGIONAL COMPETITION, then
it's the TALENT SHOW... Oh, yes, and I still haven't got
the COSTUMES FROM GRANNY.

HELP!

You called?

Fairy
godmother!

Before we leave, Dad loads
up the car – he is packing
his MOST spangly karaoke
cardigans.

"Of course, it really is all
about the sound," he
whispers (he has been
whispering for a week to protect
his voice). "But, hey, you might as
well look good too, eh?" He then smiles
a smile so wide it looks like it might hurt!

"Granny said she has only just finished
the costumes," I remind Mum. "We
need to pick them up."

"I've got a better idea,"
replies Mum. "I'll ask Sonia
to fetch them."

This is a **TERRIBLE** idea. It gives Sonia the perfect opportunity to 'LOSE' our costumes! I have to stop her from sabotaging our show!

"Let me speak to Sonia," I say. I need to send her as far away from the talent show as possible. I explain to her I need a special wig comb from the costume shop at the far end of town – that should keep her busy!

Weird wig comb

We're finally all in the car. Mabel seems strangely upbeat.

"So, will Richard join us for karaoke?" asks Mum.

Upbeat Mabel? I'm SUSPICIOUS!

"Of course, he is a huge fan of Dad's singing,"
says Mabel.

Strangely, he is not such a big fan of my acting, but then
he isn't interested in SUCKING UP TO ME.

For once dad's singing is not disturbing us in the car as
he 'saves his voice', and we are soon pulling up to the
venue of the regional final...

"Captain Fong's Kitchen," says my dad in a quiet,
awe-struck voice. "This, my beloved family, is where my
singing career is going to take off!"

There is a large crowd gathered as we enter the restaurant. It's by far the biggest buffet in town and we all pile up our plates.

"Have a good lunch, Beth," says my mum. "You'll be straight on stage after this." She lowers her voice... "And you'd better not have brought that pet with you."

I wish I *had* brought Scribbles with me, as he could have helped me clear my plate. Because the food is **TERRIBLE**, but leaving it is not an option.

Richard has arrived and he has spotted that the people who will be judging the competition are sitting at the next table – and they all seem to be really enjoying the food.

"Eat up!" says Mum, trying to sound as cheerful as possible.

Me, limp?!

I soldier through my limp Peking duck and wrestle my way through a pile of bitter pak choi, but I then hit an immoveable object. A food stuff so unpleasant I simply cannot, will not, SHALL NOT EAT IT...

The next page is NOT NICE!

Prepare for the terror of...

SLIMY NOODLES!

These are so oily and sticky that even for the sake of my dad's singing career I can't eat them.

But with the judges watching, we need to pretend we like the food. I need to get rid of these noodles, fast. I work through some solutions to unwanted noodles:

I could use my WITCH skills to conjure up a

noodle-eating dragon...

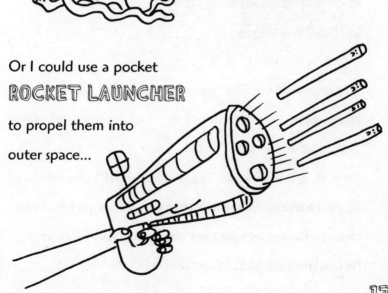

Yikes!

Or I could use a pocket

ROCKET LAUNCHER

to propel them into

outer space...

But finally I decide the simplest thing is to stuff them into my pocket when no one is looking. It's not very nice, but it's for Dad's singing career, after all.

Fortunately, no one notices as Richard and Mabel are making so much noise laughing at each other's jokes, and Mum is busy helping Bertie to eat (wisely, he thinks the best thing to do with Captain Fong's food is to throw it around).

"Delicious!" I say in a loud voice, showing off my empty plate.

"Yes, that was an... er... remarkable meal," says my mum as she crunches something that was meant to be chewy, then chews something that was meant to be crunchy (it really is that kind of restaurant).

It is now time for the singing to start and our tables are quickly cleared and the lights are dimmed.

There is a buzz of excitement in the room as, one by one, the singers take to the stage.

"They are better than the singers at the Red Emperor," whispers my mum. "But not better than your father."

It's time for Dad to shine. As he takes to the stage our table goes mad, cheering and clapping. But as the music starts...

There's nothing. Dad seems to have a frog in his throat –
in fact, make that a frog's leg, two beef dumplings and
a portion of sweet and sour chicken.

We are all willing Dad on,
but he can't hit the high notes.

Then I remember – the golf ball at the Musgrove party!
When he tripped, his high note almost shattered a
chandelier. If only I had a golf ball...

Then I see the answer, on Bertie's plate. In the form of
an inedible PRAWN BALL.

I roll it onto the stage...

"Dad! Come here!" I whisper loudly.

Looking confused, my dad
starts to walk over – and

SLIPS
ON THE
PRAWN
BALL!

He hits the high notes
– the crowd goes wild!
After that, he sings on like
he has never sung before.

He has done it – Dad has won!

BRAVO!

WONDERFUL!

CLAP!
CLAP!
CLAP!

MORE!

"Thanks for your support, guys," booms my dad, who is now back at full volume. "Who's for pudding?"

The puddings look even worse than the main courses.

Something floating in something else... Help!

Has everyone forgotten the TALENT SHOW?
I am in a huge hurry, but nobody else in my family
seems to have noticed...

Dad is joking with his fellow contestants and having his
picture taken for the local paper...

Mabel and Richard seem to be – wait for it –
smooching by the crispy wontons trolley.

"Mum, the TALENT SHOW!" I finally yell. Mum turns completely pale. Dad tucks his trophy under his arm and waves goodbye, muttering about not being the only 'star in the family'.

"I can't believe I nearly forgot!" Mum gasps. "Sorry, Beth!"

Outside the restaurant, there is no sign of Sonia. Not surprising, as she is currently looking for an imaginary wig comb at a shop that's miles away.

"She promised to fetch the costumes from Granny," says Mum.

"It's not like her at all," says Dad. "She's so efficient." Of course I know what's happening, and take charge of the situation.

"Not a problem," I say. "Mum, you get a taxi to the school and I will pick up the costumes with Dad."

With Sonia off the scene and unable to ruin my act, we are FINALLY heading over to Granny's.

"Let's hope she hasn't forgotten to make them," chuckles Dad as we approach Granny's house.

Granny's house! Yay!

"Yeah, just imagine appearing in front of the whole school in your undies!" howls Mabel.

"Almost as embarrassing as snogging in a Chinese restaurant," I reply.

But it's no good – now the image of me singing in my pants is stuck in my head. Maybe sending Sonia away wasn't such a good idea after all...

But when we get there, Granny is at the door to meet us, clutching what looks like a huge pack of DOGS!

Hello dearie!

"Well, you said you wanted to look like werewolves," said Granny, as my dad puts the costumes in the back of the car.

But Granny has clearly never seen Dusk Light because with these we're going to look more like zoo animals than super-cool werewolves.

Still, they are a lot better than anything I could have done and will probably look AMAZING when they are on...

"Thanks, Granny," I say. "And what about the Goldilocks outfit?"

"That's why there was a delay," says Granny, reaching for my second outfit. "Otto got a bit 'annoyed' by it. And, well, it's a bit...pecked."

"No Goldilocks outfit?" I cry.

"No, I did make you an outfit, but it was all a bit of a rush. I had to use the materials I had in the house."

This sounds WORRYING.

"In the end I had to use one of my old cushions," says Granny, handing me a home-made leotard. "It was a leopard print cushion, very fashionable back in my day."

It is going to look RIDICULOUS. This is not Goldilocksy AT ALL. But I don't have time to discuss it.

"Thank you, Granny," I say. At least I'll look like Goldilocks with my long blonde wig.

'You're welcome. Now, who wants a lovely slice of Strawberry Wall cake?' says Granny, beaming.

A bit closer, Terry, I can't reach the strawberries!

Strawberry Wall cake is an old favourite and is GORGEOUS – full of strawberries and, you guessed it, it's as big as a wall.

I can see my dad is tempted but fortunately Otto

decides to attack his trophy and that gets us on our way.

Tasty trophy!
Tasty trophy!

"Make sure you film it for me!" shouts Granny

as we zoom off.

We are finally heading in the direction of the theatre...

and I am now in a calm place.

They're a bit weird but I've got the costumes, and

I know my sketch off by heart.

OK, so we won't be the earliest there, but

what else could possibly go wrong?*

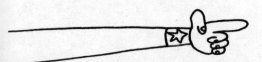

*I already wish I hadn't asked that question.

Because soon **EVERYTHING** goes wrong.

First of all, the theatre car park is FULL. That means jumping out of the car and grabbing all the bags of costumes.

"I'll park and see you in there," says Dad as he screeches off.

Mabel, Richard and I scramble past a long queue of people waiting to get in.

OK, perhaps there weren't trolls and dragons in the queue!

So here I am. The town theatre. And in big lights it reads:

TONIGHT, SCHOOL TALENT SHOW!

It feels like there are about 1000 moths in my tummy, all fluttering about having a noisy party!

As Richard and Mabel go to take their seats, I quickly

dash in through the stage door (the special entrance

that only people in the show get to use).

When I get in I meet my mum.

She has a clipboard and is in a

SERIOUS FLUSTER.

"We're running ten minutes late, Anju's

roller-skating routine is completely out of control and

one of the girls has got severe stage fright..." says Mum.

"But you're just in time!"

Cordy and Izzy are in the changing room, waiting for me

and the costumes.

"We thought perhaps you'd been attacked by ninja

spring rolls," says Cordy, as she starts to pull the outfits

out of the bag.

"These are amazing!" says Izzy, as they see the werewolf outfits that Granny has made.

"Hey, look, there's even a furry plaster-cast cover!" says Cordy as she puts her costume on.

Ms Hailey, who is introducing the acts, now pokes her head into the changing room (dressed in a big frilly outfit that seems to involve a lot of feathers).

She's followed by a
miserable-looking Team Tutu.

"We can't go on without
Clarissa!" Desiree wibbles.

Clarissa has STAGE FRIGHT! This I have to see...

"I'm going to be a star, I'm going to be on TV, the talent
spotter is only here to see ME," babbles Clarissa, as she
sits in the corner of the changing room, looking pale.

"I think the pressure got to her," says Mum.

"We need a lead singer!" Desiree sobs.

"I've worked too hard for this show to be ruined!"
Mum says...as SHE SQUEEZES INTO Clarissa's tutu!

"What are you doing?" I ask. But my mum has lost her
calm teacher face. "The show must go on, Beth!"

Mum! What
the-?!?

"Now don't forget the signal, Beth," says Mum. "When
you're finished, you have to raise your hands to tell me
when to come on."

We're up next! Team Howler assembles at the side of the stage.

Finally, the disco music comes to an end and Anju and her group, most of whom seem to have fallen over, take a bow and limp off the stage. There seems to be roller-skates and pompoms everywhere.

As Anju exits the stage she whispers the old showbiz expression for 'good luck': "Break a leg," she says.

Cordy doesn't see the funny side.

It's then that I look out at the audience and get that wobbly belly feeling again! I know people call it butterflies, but to me it actually feels like a miniature DIGGER is making a ditch in my tummy.

"Full house," whispers Ms Hailey. "Oh, and that's the talent spotter in the front row – he has come anonymously."

A man wearing a hat and glasses is madly taking notes. He seems strangely familiar.

But there's no time to think about it now – Ms Hailey is
already on stage, introducing us...

"Please welcome Beth, Cordy and Izzy in a sketch
entitled: Goldilocks and the Three
Werewolves!"

There is huge applause as we walk out – everyone seems
really impressed by our hairy outfits. This is going well.
As soon as we start our sketch, my nerves VANISH.

I deliver my lines and get a laugh. The crowd
LOVES our werewolf twist on the old classic.

Even my fleas
have got fleas!

Cordy gets a laugh just from limping into position, and Izzy gets a laugh when he pulls a werewolf face.

I am so confident I even sneak a look at the talent spotter to see if he's impressed... but he looks a bit unwell. Strange, I think – but the show must go on!

"OK, time for my Goldilocks change," I whisper to Izzy and Cordy. But, just as I'm about to slip off, there is a huge, scenery-shaking...

SNEEZE!

If that's not bad enough, I recognise that sneeze.

It's coming from the talent spotter – in fact, his eyes are running so much he's had to take his glasses off. And that is when I realise who it is.

I gasp out loud. "Germane DeFoot!" I gasp.

"And I'm still allergic to animals," he gasps (and his gasp is a lot louder than mine).

But there are no animals here – Scribbles doesn't enjoy the theatre.

I prefer the opera.

Mr DeFoot is pointing at my outfit. He's allergic to the fake-fur werewolf costumes! It's going horribly wrong, but we've nearly finished.

I rush backstage and quickly get into the leopard print leotard. It looks strange, but the Goldilocks wig will make it work. But it's not there!

"Mum? Have you seen my wig?" I hiss desperately. Mum is in position by the side of the stage, wearing Clarissa's outfit.

"Last time I saw it, Sonia took it to look for that wig comb you needed," Mum whispers back.

My heart sinks down so far that it's probably in Australia. What am I going to do? How can I be Goldilocks without long blonde hair?

On stage, Cordy is glancing over nervously. I'm meant to be back on stage now.

There's no time.

Then I remember something that could work as a curly wig...something slimy and unpleasant, but that could definitely work...

CAPTAIN FONG'S NOODLES!

I get them out of my trouser pocket
and arrange them as nicely
as possible on my head.

Even though the smell is terrible,
I think this is going to work.

But the audience is getting restless. I need to get
onstage, fast!

I run onto the stage but the noodles are in my eyes and
I trip over something.

I'm a chopstick, and
you just don't do
that to noodles!

"My leg!" cries Cordy. "That hurt more than when the alien broke it!" But as I'm trying to regain my footing I now seem to be gaining speed at an alarming rate.

I'm on a roller-skate from Anju's roller-disco routine!

As I fly across the stage I lose control of my arms, waving them in the air. This is a BIG problem, because my mum thinks I have given the signal for Team Tutu to start. I can't stop her! As if in slow motion, I see Mum joining me on stage and clearing her throat... and there is nothing I can do!

SO, I'm zooming across a stage in front of the whole school, wearing a leopard print leotard, I've got soggy noodles on my head –

AND MY MUM IS SINGING IN A TUTU!

I fly straight into my mum and we both tumble over. This is awful!

I need someone to get on stage, I need to do something to distract the crowd, I need...

Richard?

Yes, Mabel's boyfriend is sitting in the front row looking right at me. And he throws me a lifeline.

"Remember the end of the Lavinia book, Beth!" he shouts. "You know – when she forgets her poem."

I think back to being in the garden all those weeks ago. Then I remember, at the end of the Lavinia book, she saved the day by... singing. I turn to the audience. I need a song and quick!

As Team Tutu look at me (Desiree and Josh followed my mum onto the stage) I remember their song – and I start to sing my own version.

Team Howler is on the prowl!
Team Howler will make you growl!
We know we'll make you roar and
We'll leaving you wanting more!

Cordy and Izzy join in. We then look at Team Tutu. My mum leads the way as they pick up the song with their verse.

Team Tutu is go! Team Tutu is go! We know that we'll make it - we've got a great show! Oh, yeah!

What happens next is

EXTRAORDINARY...

The crowd LOVE IT! In fact, EVERYONE joins in. Only Clarissa is HATING it – I can see her scowling from the sidelines.

They must think the whole noodle-roller-skate-knocking-Mum-over-then-finishing-with-a-song is part of the routine...

We are all applauded off the stage!

My only regret is that Germane DeFoot, the talent spotter, wasn't there to see it. Even with one less werewolf costume onstage he still couldn't stifle the sneezes and had to leave. I later discovered he has given up talent spotting for good.

As we finally leave the theatre I see Clarissa being helped into her dad's car.

"Showbiz is for losers, anyway!" she says snootily. I should have known she wouldn't be down for long.

A few days after the talent show, and I'm back home, hanging out with Cordy.

"Thank goodness we weren't talent spotted," says Cordy. "I can't think of anything worse than having to stand up on stage every day."

"Well, at least now you *can* stand up," I say – Cordy has finally had the plaster cast removed from her leg. "So will you tell me what *really* happened? No dinosaurs or aliens, OK?"

Look, for the last time, we were **NOT INVOLVED** in the leg-breaking incident!

But before Cordy can reply there is a knock
at the door. Scribbles ducks for cover
and I quickly try to work out
what I might have done to
annoy Mabel.

But it isn't Mabel, or my mum or dad
...it's Sonia!

"Duck, hide!" I screech. "She's come to get us!"

But Sonia just looks confused as she enters my room.

"I'm so, so sorry about
your Goldilocks wig,"
she says. "I looked all
over town but I couldn't
find the shop you asked
me to go to. I'm so upset
I missed the talent show."

"It's OK," I say, feeling a bit guilty and squirmy. I feel a bit bad about suspecting her of being a spy. And after all, if I hadn't sent her away I'd have had my wig.

"Your mum's time at school has ended so you don't need a childminder any more," she says. "I've come to say goodbye."

I go and give her a hug. Maybe she wasn't so bad after all.

"While I was looking for the wig comb shop I did run into someone." She chuckles. "I'm not sure if I mentioned my last job..."

Oh dear, here it comes – so she WAS a spy!

"You mean the job with the Musgroves?" I blurt out.

"No, the job I had after that – for a couple of weeks I worked for Jamilla Stenhouse..."

"**THE** JAMILLA STENHOUSE!!!!!!!!!"

Cordy and I exclaim at the same time. As Cordy jumps up she nearly trips over.

"Careful, Cordy! You don't want to break your other leg by tripping up again!" Sonia says. "Your mum was asking me about sensible shoes..."

I'm terribly sensible!

THAT's how she broke her leg! I don't think I have ever seen it happen before, but is Cordy **BLUSHING!?!**

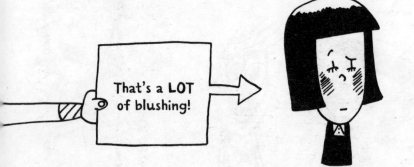

That's a LOT of blushing!

But before I can tease Cordy, Sonia interrupts.

"Anyway," she says, "Jamilla and I stayed friends, and when I bumped into her I told her you were big fans and she gave me these..."

"TWO SIGNED COPIES OF THE LATEST DUSK LIGHT NOVEL!"

we exclaim together. "Thank you, Sonia!"

Time to tell Richard and Mabel to leave the garden table – we've got some reading to do!

Read on for a

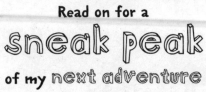

of my next adventure

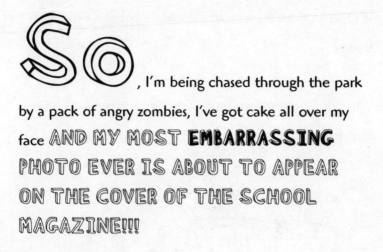

So, I'm being chased through the park by a pack of angry zombies, I've got cake all over my face AND MY MOST **EMBARRASSING** PHOTO EVER IS ABOUT TO APPEAR ON THE COVER OF THE SCHOOL MAGAZINE!!!

How did I get here? Let's go back to the beginning...

It's the weekend and today couldn't be going much better.

What do you get if you mix strawberry milkshakes, my best friend Cordy and a whole afternoon together?

(No, not a sticky mess, you get...)

GREAT TIMES.

And things are about to get EVEN better. Cordy leans in, looks around to make sure no one is listening, and says, "Do you want to hear something confidential?"

Of course I nod.

"Just you wait until you hear what I've got planned," says Cordy as she takes an extra loud schlurp on her milkshake.

I'm so excited I almost drop my extra large chocolate chip cookie (it's almost as big as a bin lid) in my milkshake.

"You're going to build that submarine out of old cereal boxes and live in a tropical paradise?" I suggest.

"That's next year." Cordy chuckles and tells me her plan.

"I'm planning..."

...my birthday party!"

"No way!" I gasp, as some milkshake comes out of my nose. "This is great news! We must make sure it's the best birthday, EVER!"

"That's the only problem," says Cordy. "I'm not sure where to have it, or what sort of cake I should get, or anything. Should I have a theme?"

"**Just leave it to me,**" I say, suddenly sounding

weirdly confident.

"I'll make sure you have the **best** birthday ever –

in fact, it'll be better than a birthday. It will be a

Bethday!"

"That would be great," says Cordy. "Are you sure?"

"Of course," I say, as my head begins to **whir** with

birthday ideas.

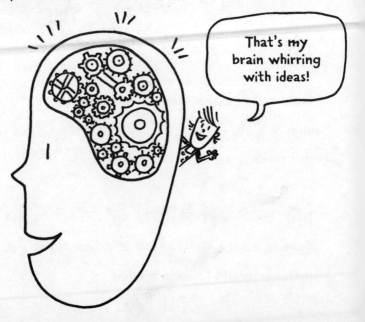

That's my
brain whirring
with ideas!

Read

BADLY DRAWN BETH:
Happy Bethday!

to find out what happens next!*

*No zombies were harmed in the making of this book.